FIRST U.S. EDITION

Library of Congress Catalog Card Number 89-83660

ISBN 0-316-04261-7

10 9 8 7 6 5 4 3 2 1

First published in 1989
in Great Britain by
William Heinemann Ltd.

Joy Street Books are
published by Little, Brown
and Company (Inc.)

Produced by Mandarin Offset
Printed and bound in Hong Kong

Tom's Rainbow Walk

Catherine Anholt

JOY STREET BOOKS

Little, Brown and Company
Boston · Toronto · London

"Time for a nap, Tom," said Grandma,
"and while you're asleep I'll knit you
a beautiful new sweater."

"What color would you like?"
"Red, please," said Tom, "it's my favorite.
Or maybe green. But I like blue, too,
and yellow is nice . . ."

Before Tom had chosen a color,
he fell asleep. In his dream
he saw a huge ball of yarn.

"Where is it going?" he wondered.
He chased it down the steps
into Grandma's garden.

The yarn rolled right up to the pond
where two foxes sat fishing.
"Hello," said Tom. "Can you help me
choose a color for my new sweater?"
"That's easy," said the foxes. "Red is
the best color, just like our fur coats."
"Thanks," said Tom. "I think I'd
like a red sweater."

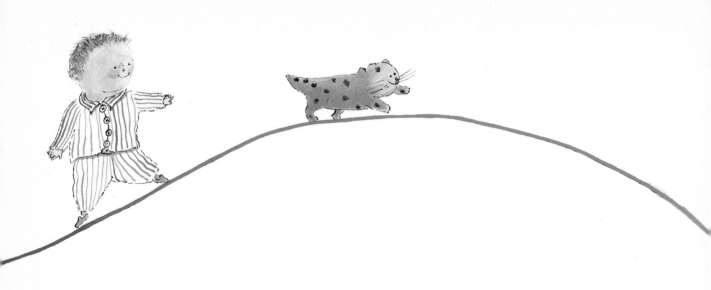

Tom ran on until he found some
little chicks playing in the yard.
"Hey, chicks," he called.
"What color do *you* think my
new sweater should be?"
"We like yellow," they cheeped.
"Maybe they're right," thought Tom.
"I do like their fluffy yellow feathers."

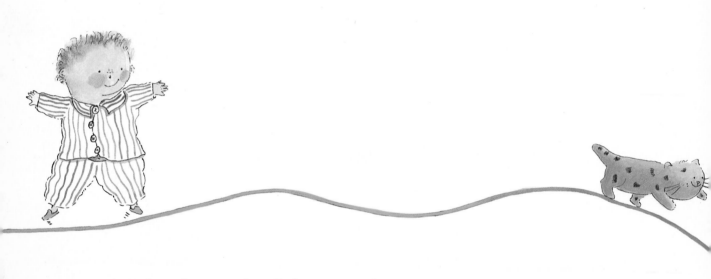

At the far end of the pond
a family of frogs were hopping about.
"What's your favorite color, frogs?" called Tom.
"Green, green, green," they croaked.
"I like green, too," said Tom.

Just then a big blue fish
popped out of the water.
"If you're looking for a color
and you don't know what to do,
choose any color of the rainbow,
as long as it is blue," he called.
"That's it," said Tom,
"blue is a good color for a sweater."

Tom skipped down to the vegetable patch
where a large pig was sitting
in a wheelbarrow eating grapes.
"What color should my new sweater be?"
called Tom.
"Try purple like these juicy grapes,
or pink like me," said the pig.
"Hmmm," said Tom. "I like both pink and purple.

Before he knew it, Tom had walked
all around Grandma's garden
and back to the house.
A rooster was perched on the windowsill.
"Cock-a-doodle-do," he crowed,
"What will you do?"
"Choose *all* the colors of the rainbow," cried Tom,
"not just one or two!"

As soon as Tom woke up,
he called out to Grandma.

But Grandma had just finished
knitting his sweater.
And it was red as a fox,
yellow as a chick,
green as a frog,
blue as a fish,
pink as a pig
and as colorful as a rooster.
It fit perfectly!